Hello, Bingo!

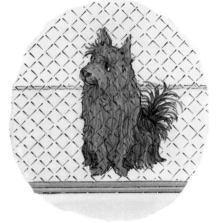

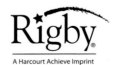

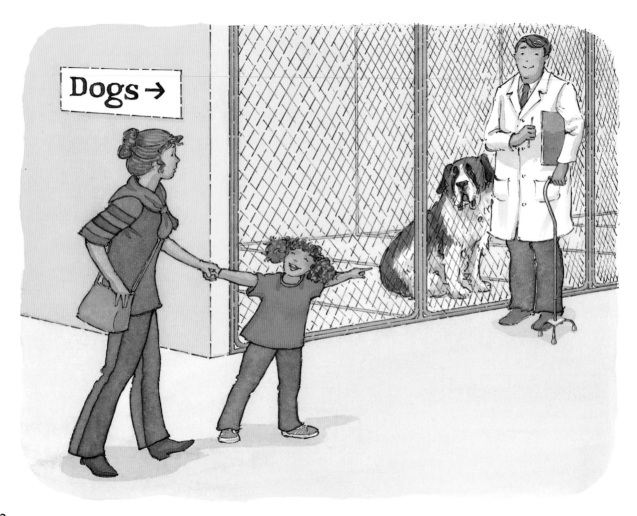

Dogs →

"Come and look at the dogs,"

said Sam.

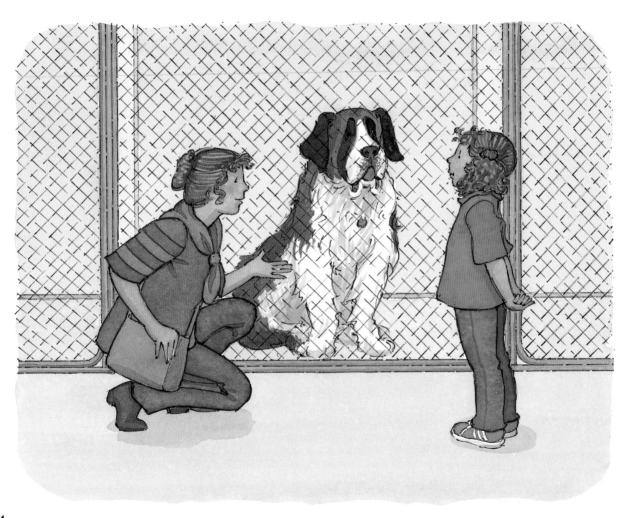

"Here is a big dog,"

said Mom.

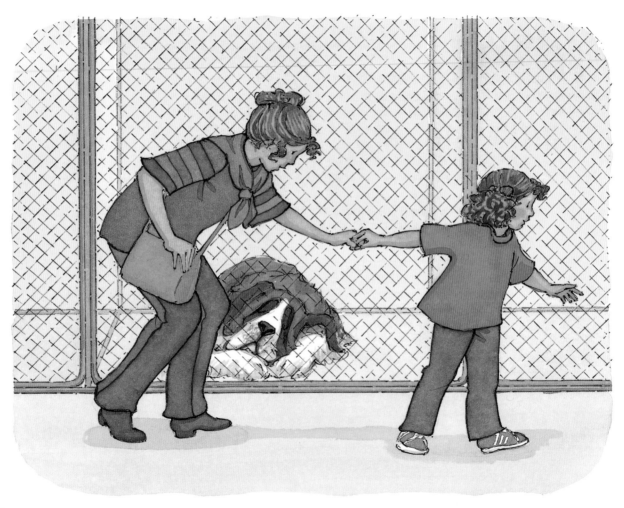

"No," said Sam.

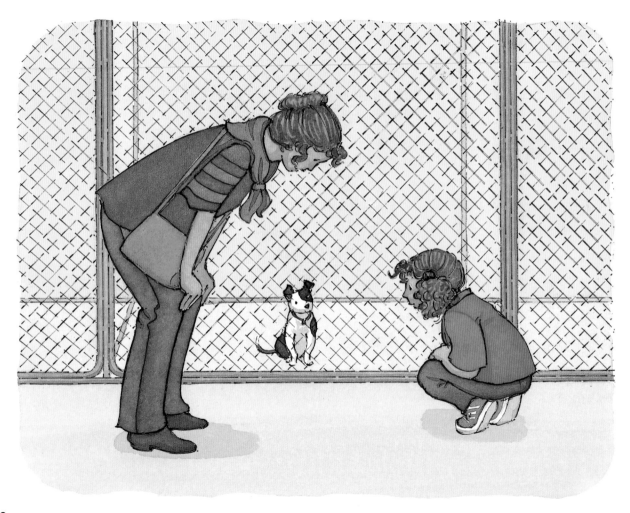

"Here is a little dog,"

said Mom.

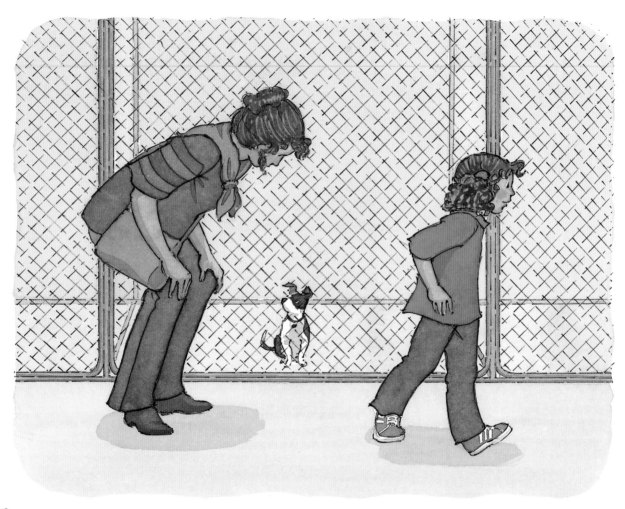

"No," said Sam.

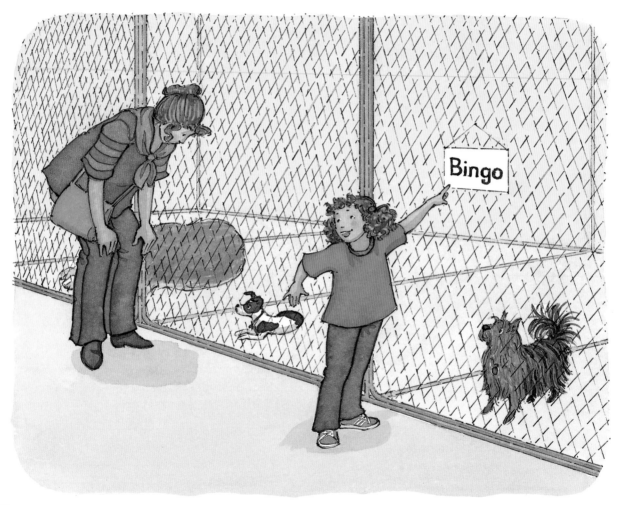

"Here is Bingo," said Sam.

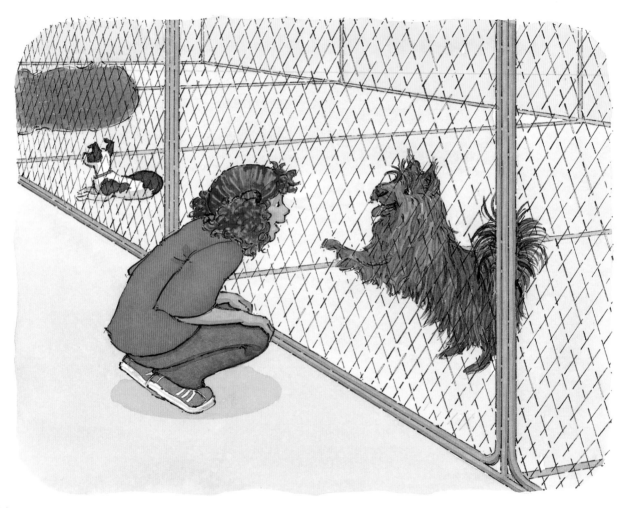

"Come and look at Bingo."

"Hello, Bingo!" said Sam.

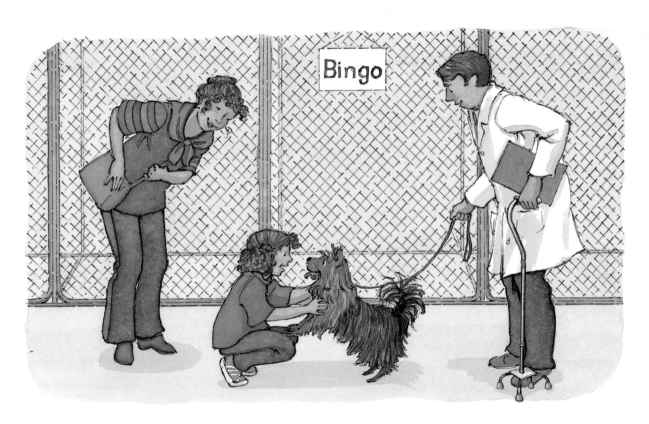